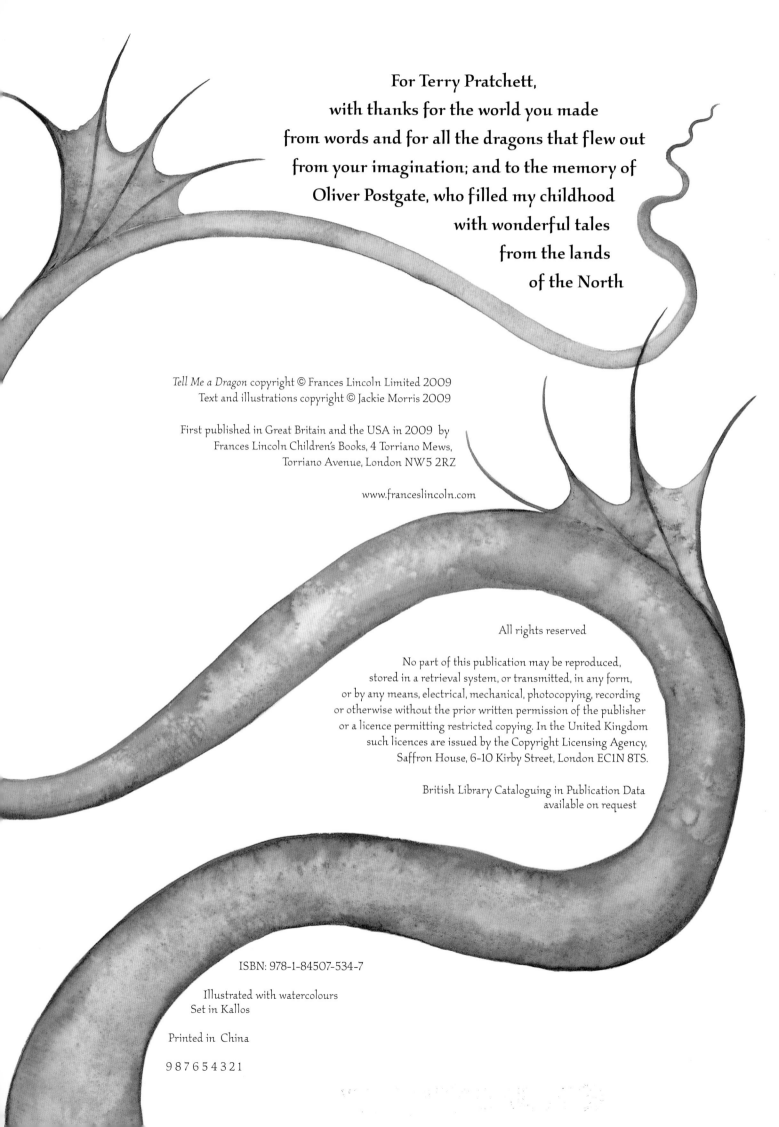

For Terry Pratchett,
with thanks for the world you made
from words and for all the dragons that flew out
from your imagination; and to the memory of
Oliver Postgate, who filled my childhood
with wonderful tales
from the lands
of the North

Tell Me a Dragon copyright © Frances Lincoln Limited 2009
Text and illustrations copyright © Jackie Morris 2009

First published in Great Britain and the USA in 2009 by
Frances Lincoln Children's Books, 4 Torriano Mews,
Torriano Avenue, London NW5 2RZ

www.franceslincoln.com

British Library Cataloguing in Publication Data
available on request

ISBN: 978-1-84507-534-7

Illustrated with watercolours
Set in Kallos

Printed in China

9 8 7 6 5 4 3 2 1

JACKIE MORRIS

TELL ME A DRAGON

F

FRANCES LINCOLN
CHILDREN'S BOOKS

My dragon is made from the sun and the stars.
Sparkled with stardust,
all night he follows the silver moon-path
across the sky.

My dragon eats
sweet, perfumed flowers.
When she laughs,
petals ride on her breath.

My dragon is snaggle-toothed, fierce and brave.

My dragon is as big as a village,
jade-winged and amber-eyed
with a tail as long as a river.

My dragons are tiny,

with whisper-thin wings of rainbow hues.

My dragon is a sky dragon.
Together we ride to the secret music of the wind.

My dragon is a **sea-dragon**.
All day he plays,
racing dolphins in the waves.

My dragon is a fire dragon.
His heart is always warm.

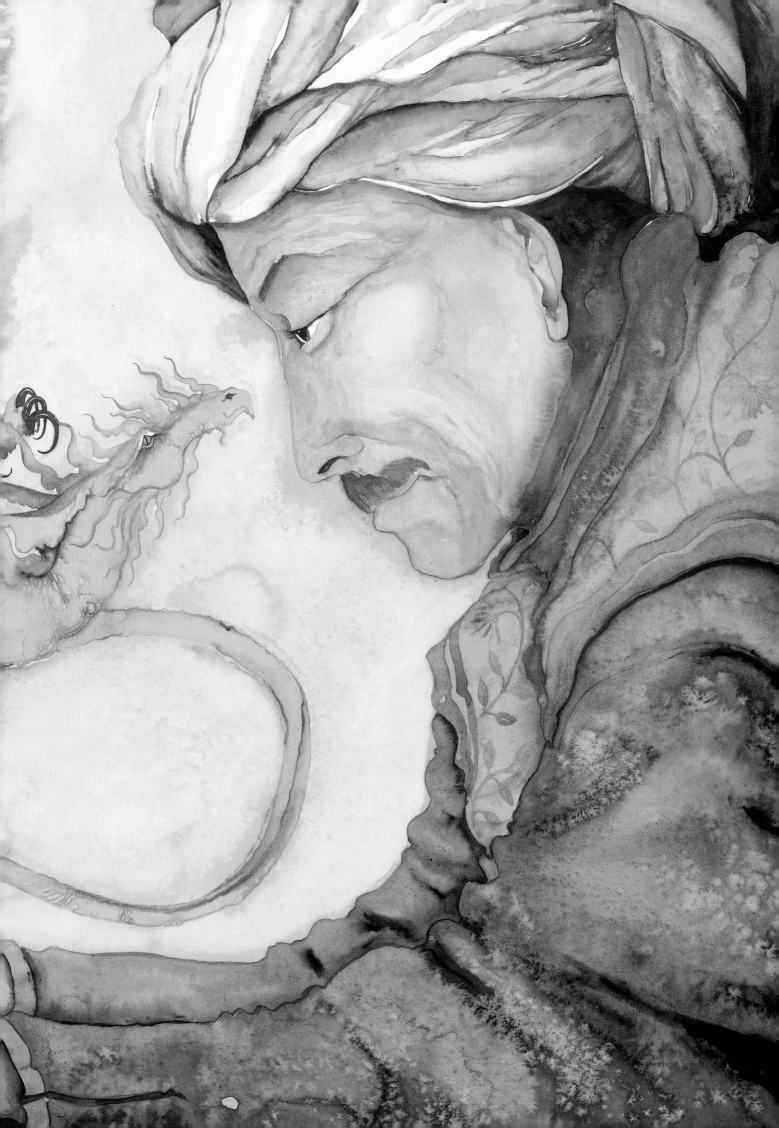

My dragon is an ice-dragon. His breath is snowflakes.

Curled around my ear, my dragon sings sweet songs
and tells me strange stories
from far away
and long ago.

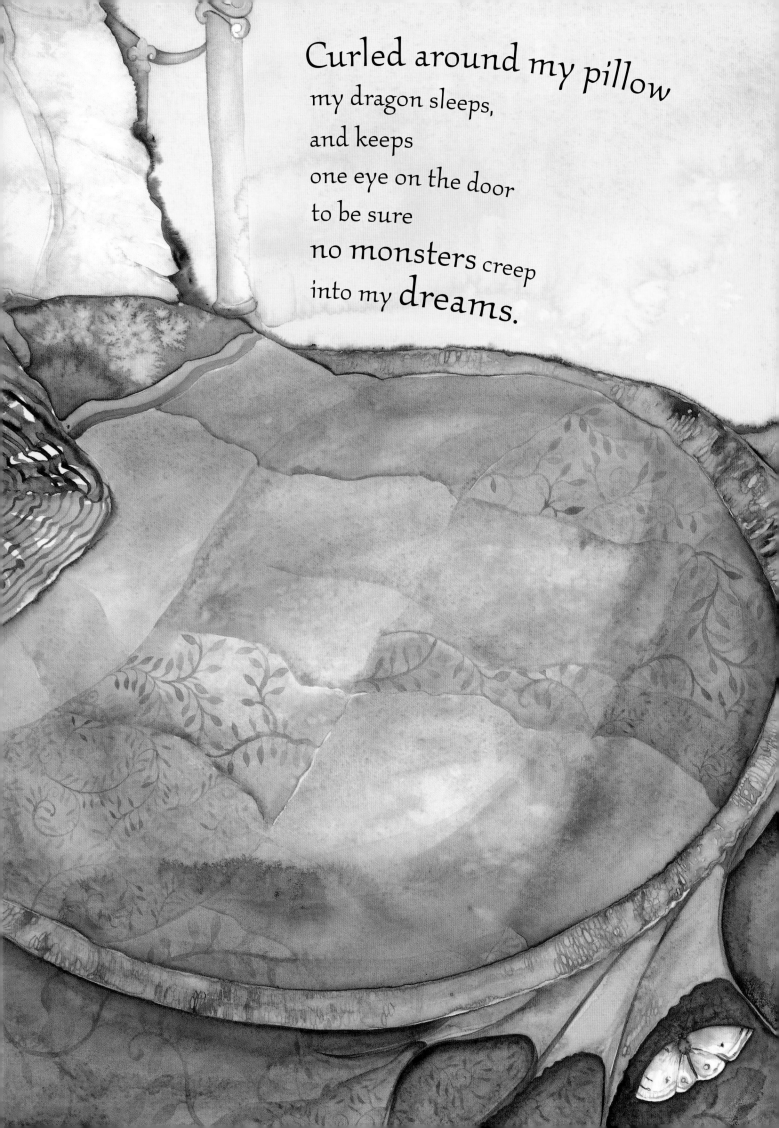

Curled around my pillow
my dragon sleeps,
and keeps
one eye on the door
to be sure
no monsters creep
into my dreams.

Tell me about your dragon.